Hiking Day

BY *Anne Rockwell*

ILLUSTRATED BY *Lizzy Rockwell*

ALADDIN • New York • London • Toronto • Sydney • New Delhi

for Ayla Akemi

Today my mother, my father, and I are going to climb Hickory Hill.

That's the mountain I see from my window.

It looks like a mountain to me, but everyone calls it Hickory Hill.

I put on sturdy sneakers,
find my floppy hat,
and fill my water bottle.

The ride from our house to Hickory Hill
takes about twenty minutes.

As we drive, I see fewer and fewer houses
and more and more tall trees.

As soon as we park the car, we check the map to see which trail to follow.

Trails are like paths cut through the woods.

We choose the red one—it's my favorite color.

The minute we step onto the trail, we are surrounded by tall trees.

We can't see sky.

The ground is covered with leaves and ferns.

It looks like the inside of my mother's terrarium.

It is so quiet.

I can hear my sneakers crunching the ground.

As we climb higher up Hickory Hill, a fat toad leaps in front of us.

"Ribbit, ribbit!" he says.

I kneel down to look at him.

His colors match the floor of the woods and the tree bark.

"Hey," says my father. "Where is the red trail marker?"

"Uh-oh," Mom says. "Where can it be?"

Are we lost? I wonder.

We look at all the tree trunks around us. Then we notice a prickly porcupine slowly climbing a tree. As she moves up the trunk, I see a red mark appear.

"I found it!" I cry.

We begin hiking again.

I hear a loud *tap, tap, tap. Tap, tap, tap.*

It sounds like someone is using a hammer!

A little chipmunk puts a hickory nut in her mouth and scurries through the leaves.

"Getting ready for winter," my father says.

The *tap, tap, tap* gets louder.

My mother points up, and I see a woodpecker making a hole in a tree.

"He is looking for insects hiding inside," she tells me. "He uses his beak to make the hole bigger and find good things to eat."

"Bugs? Yuck!" say Dad and I.

We see some yellow mushrooms and red berries growing on a bush.

But that beautiful, friendly toad is gone.

Maybe he decided to hike down Hickory Hill instead of hiking up with us.

Soon we stop for a drink.

All of a sudden I know someone is looking at me.

I slowly turn to see a deer with wide antlers.

He leaps away so fast that no one sees him but me.

The more we walk, the more I notice the trees are not so tall.

The ground is rockier.

Now I can see bits of blue sky, and even an airplane flying across the sky.

Suddenly the ground below my feet
isn't the woodland floor.

It is a big, flat rock.

"We're at the summit," my father tells me.
"The top of Hickory Hill!"

"We did it!" I say.

We all sit down on the sunny, warm rock, and guess who jumps up to be with us?

The friendly, fat toad!

ALADDIN

An imprint of Simon & Schuster Children's Publishing Division

1230 Avenue of the Americas, New York, New York 10020

First Aladdin paperback edition November 2020

Text copyright © 2018 by Anne Rockwell

Illustrations copyright © 2018 by Lizzy Rockwell

Also available in an Aladdin hardcover edition.

For information about special discounts for bulk purchases, please contact

Simon & Schuster Special Sales at 1-866-506-1949 or business@simonandschuster.com.

The Simon & Schuster Speakers Bureau can bring authors to your live event. For more

information or to book an event contact the Simon & Schuster Speakers Bureau

at 1-866-248-3049 or visit our website at www.simonspeakers.com.

Designed by Jessica Handelman

The illustrations for this book were rendered in watercolor.

The text of this book was set in Caslon.

Manufactured in China 0820 SCP

10 9 8 7 6 5 4 3 2 1

Library of Congress Control Number 2017956447

ISBN 978-1-4814-2737-1 (hc)

ISBN 978-1-4814-2738-8 (pbk)

ISBN 978-1-4814-2739-5 (eBook)